Danny Follows the Signs

written and photographed
by
Mia Coulton

Danny looked at the sign on the tree.

COME PLAY IN THE PARK
OPENS TODAY

3

COME PLAY IN THE PARK
OPENS TODAY

"Look Norman, the sign has a map to the park. Let's go!" said Danny.

"This way!" said Norman.

"Slow down!" said Danny.

"The sign says SLOW."

"This way!" said Norman.

"We have to stop
at the sign," said Danny.
"The sign says to STOP!"

"Come here!

This is the way we go

to the park!" said Norman.

"Oh, no!" said Danny. "The sign says we must be on a leash."

"You stay here.

I will be right back,"

said Danny.

"Now we can go play in the park," said Danny.